LITTLE MISS WISE

Roger Hargreaves

D1513182

Original concept by
Roger Hargreaves

EGMONT

Little Miss Wise was as wise as an owl.

Possibly two owls.

Being so wise and sensible meant that Little Miss Wise
brushed her teeth every day,
made her bed every day,
tidied her house every day,
and did lots of other wise and sensible things.

If you are as wise and sensible as Little Miss Wise,
you'll know just what kind of other things she did.

Little Miss Wise liked to go for a walk every day.

A walk that was neither too long, nor too short.

A walk that was wise and sensible.

Or sensible and wise, if you prefer.

On her walks she often met other people.

People who were not quite so wise.

And sometimes, people who were decidedly unwise.

Last Monday she met Little Miss Naughty.

"Come and jump in the puddles!" cried Little Miss Naughty, with a naughty gleam in her eye.

But Little Miss Wise, being wise, refused.

She didn't want to get HER feet wet.

On Tuesday she met Little Miss Greedy, who was carrying an enormous cake filled with cream and smothered with pink icing.

"Would you like some of this?" asked Little Miss Greedy.

Little Miss Wise refused.

She didn't want an upset stomach.

On Wednesday Little Miss Wise refused to get into Mr Busy's racing car.

She didn't want to have an accident.

On Thursday she refused to go into Mr Messy's house.

"If I go into his house, I will get dirty," she said to herself.

But she didn't say anything to Mr Messy.

She didn't want to hurt his feelings.

On Friday she refused to play tennis with Mr Silly.

There's nothing silly about that, is there?

By Saturday, Little Miss Wise was feeling unhappy.

"If I keep saying 'No' all the time, I'll upset everybody and I won't have any friends left," she said to herself.

She thought long and hard about the problem and, being the wise and sensible person she is, she came up with an answer.

"From now on, I will say 'Yes' to everything."

On Sunday, while she was out on one of her wise and sensible walks, or sensible and wise walks, if you prefer, Little Miss Wise met Mr Mischief.

He was carrying a parcel.

"Please accept this small present," he said to her.

"N ..." began Little Miss Wise.

But then she remembered her decision.

"Yes! Thank you!" she cried.

She took the parcel.

And off skipped Mr Mischief, with a mischievous grin on his face.

Little Miss Wise opened the parcel.

"ATISHOO!" she sneezed.

Then she sneezed again.

And she sneezed, and sneezed, and sneezed
all day long.

She used one hundred and ninety-nine handkerchiefs.

Mr Mischief's present had been sneezing powder!